VEDA KEDA

Periwinkle

To my own heartbreak.

I

PARIS

When your soft eyes meet hers, smile
So she can smile, hey what's up beauty, talk to her

THE MANUAL — EDDY KIM

PARIS, FRANCE

There was always something about lights that always beckoned Joanna. The lights were some sort of relief— a breath of fresh air that swept through her lungs and in a way rejuvenated her. She felt alive amongst the shimmering lights, and she felt alive with him.

The first time they met was in front of the Eiffel Tower at night. He was there for his report; she was there to look at the pretty lights. He was studying journalism and flew out to Paris to get an opinion article for his assignment. Joanna, on the other hand, just moved to Paris for the semester to study fashion. That was her dream— to be a fashion designer.

In a way, Joanna thought it was fate that brought her to Paris. She barely got accepted into the study abroad program, and while she was sad that she had to leave her friends behind, she just barely avoided a run in with an abusive former lover who was searching for her in her apartment complex as she was sitting on the airplane. She barely made it, but she made it, and it was everything she had ever hoped for.

It was the first semester of her final year for Joanna when she arrived in Paris. She actually should've gone to Paris during her junior year. However, she lacked the funds to be able to go to Paris— not to mention, she failed to qualify for the program due to a missing credit— so she had to go her senior year. She didn't mind, though, because she was thrilled at the chance to just be in Paris and study fashion. The sad thing was that she was so busy working on her final projects that she didn't even get to go sightseeing at touristy locations until her last month in Paris.

"Dahlia, I'm telling you, this place is just so romantic. Wouldn't it be great if I found my soulmate here?" Joanna breathed out as she talked on the phone with her best friend.

"Wow, imagine you and a French guy! You two would have the cutest babies," Joanna heard her friend giggle.

"I can't believe it's my last month here, though. I'm finally going to see the Eiffel Tower," Joanna whined as she continued at a quick pace.

"Jesus, college really does suck the life out of studying abroad, doesn't it," Dahlia laughed before sighing painfully.

"Anyway," Joanna started to chuckle before getting abruptly interrupted by her violent shivering. "I'm supposed to meet up with some friends and take pictures, but it's so cold out!"

"Do it for the pretty lights. Suffer for the pretty lights," Dahlia said. "God, I have to go. I have class now. Bye! Have fun!"

"Thank you! Talk to you later," Joanna responded before hanging the phone up.

Joanna put her phone in her pocket and saw her three friends waving her over. She caught up and walked with them to the Eiffel Tower. It was dark outside, and the first thing she saw was the sparkling lights of the tower. She exhaled softly and smiled— the tower was beautiful. She broke off from the group to take pictures of just the tower for Dahlia. Once she got some good pictures, she turned to return to her friends, only to notice that they were busy giggling. She walked over to them with a perplexed look on her face.

"What's up?" Joanna asked them.

"We want to ask that cute guy to take pictures of us, but we're—" one of her friends started.

"Joanna! You should ask him to take pictures of us!" another one of her friends interrupted. as her third friend pushed her from behind.

"Wait! I don't—"

Before she could even argue, Joanna's third friend pushed her from behind towards the boy. She found herself within close proximity of the cute boy while her friends ran away and stood off to the side while continuing to giggle. She huffed in frustration. Although she had told Dahlia that she wanted to find her soulmate here, she really didn't want to be forced to talk to a boy. After mustering up her courage for a good couple of seconds, Joanna went up to the guy and asked in her best French, "Excuse me, could you take pictures of me and my friends in front of the tower?"

The boy turned around, and Joanna could've sworn she was hit in the stomach with a bat because she lost all wind. He was gorgeous. His hair seemed to fall into place just perfectly, and his eyes sparkled as if the lights of the tower were in his own eyes. His features felt unreal— as if a Renaissance painter delicately painted his soft features on his face. He had soft rosy lips that matched the light blush that dusted his face from the cold wind circulating around the French lights. He smiled softly as he completely turned his body towards the short girl, and for a second, Joanna forgot how to breath.

"I'm sorry, I don't speak French," he said in fluent English, the words rolling off his tongue like water droplets on an ice cold beverage sitting outside in the hot summer sun.

"That's okay," Joanna finally managed to quickly relearn how to breathe as she responded in English.

There was a beat of silence between them as Joanna couldn't help but to continue to stare at the lovely features on the stranger's face. She lost all sense of shame as she continued to observe his face. Two little moles dotted his cheek which rose every time he smiled. For some reason, he seemed to sparkle every time he moved, and Joanna didn't know if it was because of the lights around him or if he really was that brilliant.

"May I help you with something?" he snapped her out of her thoughts.

"I just wanted to know if you could take a picture with me— I mean of me and my friends!" Joanna stuttered out.

The boy laughed and said, "Sure, I can take a picture with you and then of you and your friends."

"What?" Joanna was confused.

The boy reached for Joanna's phone and slipped the phone out of her hand. He stepped closer to her and wrapped his hand around her shoulder as he opened the camera on her phone and proceeded to take a picture with her. Joanna ended up smiling last second because she was too flustered to realize her current situation. He took the picture then beckoned for her friends so that she could take pictures with her friends at the Eiffel Tower.

"Thank you so much," Joanna told him as she received her phone from him.

"Wait, I want that picture I took with you. Here's my name and number," he handed Joanna a card. "Send it to me when you can."

She thanked him again and promised him that she would send the picture to him. She then returned to her friends and got an earful about how the cute boy gave her his number and took a freaking selfie with her. She laughed it off, but as she and her friends headed back to the dorm, she looked at his card. His name, his job, and his number were all on there. Joanna kept staring at the card as she and her friends walked back to their dorms. She wanted to say his name out loud, but she was already embarrassed enough by her friends forcing her to talk to him, so she just stayed silent on the way back home.

His name was Christian Lee. He was a journalist based in the fashion industry. Joanna recognized the company he worked for. She was astonished. On one hand, she really wanted to maintain a friendship with him just to get her ahead in the industry, but on the other hand, she really liked him and wanted more than just a friendship. She tucked the business card in her phone case and smiled to herself. She was excited. When she got back to the dorm, she sent the photo to him and went to bed. The next morning when she woke up, she saw that he texted her back.

Joanna blushed as she read the messages. He thanked her and then told her that she was pretty. She responded to him, the more she kept talking to him, the more she liked him. By the time she managed to get herself out of bed, she had planned a date for later that day with him. She didn't tell any of her college friends, but she did tell June about her current situation because she needed help with deciding what to wear.

"I was thinking this black skirt with tights and this peach blouse, but should I even wear a skirt?" she asked Dahlia as she facetimed her.

"What were you wearing when you first met him?" Dahlia inquired.

"It doesn't matter because I was wearing a big jacket over it," Joanna sighed. "Anyway, is the skirt too much?"

"I think the skirt is fine, but wear that white button-up you have with that fancy necklace," Dahlia said as she pointed on the screen.

Joanna nodded and grabbed the shirt. She got changed and wore her accessories in the bathroom before fixing her hair. She considered leaving it down, but she also thought a high ponytail would look better with the outfit. She ended up putting her hair up. She was already wearing makeup, so now all that was left was to find a cute pair of shoes to match her outfit.

"Thanks, Dahlia," Joanna said after she got dressed. "I'm going to go now."

"Good luck on your date!" Dahlia wished her before Joanna hung up.

Turns out Christian chose to meet up at a coffee shop right by the Eiffel Tower, and it just so happened to be the coffee shop Joanna really wanted to go to. Joanna thought she was going to get to the coffee shop first, but Christian ended up getting there ahead of time because he had to do a couple of interviews in the area.

Joanna was fascinated by Christian. During the entire date, she couldn't even comprehend a word he was saying. She was so infatuated with the shape of his eyes, the way his lips curled when he smiled, and the way he kept running his hands through his hair. He seemed so perfect.

After they finished having coffee, Christian and Joanna took a stroll on the streets of Paris. Joanna tried to keep her hands to herself as they walked side by side and enjoyed window shopping, but at some point during their walk, Christian's hand brushed past Joanna's fingers. She felt a light blush pop onto her face as Christian's pinky finger wrapped around her own pinky. She looked up at him and saw a small smile on his face. Joanna looked down at her moving feet flustered. She felt his fingers lace with hers. He gave her hand a gentle, reassuring squeeze. Joanna felt hot even though it was freezing outside.

The second time the two met up, Christian and Joanna got crêpes together. As she was eating, Joanna got some of the whipped cream from the strawberry crêpe she ordered on her nose. Before she could wipe the cream off of her nose, Christian licked the cream off of her nose. Joanna considered slapping the boy, but as she raised her hand, Christian laughed and ran away from the girl. They spent the rest of the day chasing each other and laughing. It had been a while since Joanna had that much fun with someone she just met.

The first time Christian kissed Joanna was on their third date. His kiss tasted like brown sugar and caramel in a warm drink— it was almost too sweet for her. She felt herself drowning in his embrace, in his kiss. She wanted his soft lips not only on her lips, but on her cheek, her neck, trailing down to her collarbones and leaving painful purple marks all over her chest. She pulled him towards her as they made out. They were sitting— now laying— on the couch in Christian's apartment. Joanna could feel her limbs turn to putty as Christian trailed his nose down her neck and to her chest. He slowly unbuttoned her light pink blouse and trailed a finger down the center of her torso. Joanna's back arched in pleasure. Her phone then rang, and Joanna had to rush back to her dorm to video chat with her mother. While she regretted running out of his apartment like that, she knew that the moment would happen between them as long as she remained patient.

After a week, the two went on their fourth date. Joanna attempted to make food for Christian, but she nearly burned down the kitchen in her dorm room, so they ended up going out for Italian food in the middle of Paris. He gave her a pendant that she had been looking at ever since the two of them started going out. It was a small, golden marigold dangling on a thin, gold chain. She thanked him for the necklace, and in response, he kissed her on the cheek and smiled at her. Joanna honestly expected them to go further that night, but Christian ended up kissing her in front of the building of her dorm and left. She was slightly disappointed, but they had made plans for another date later that week, so she could make her move then.

Joanna and Christian didn't even make their dinner reservations on their fifth date. Dahlia advised Joanna to wear her most flattering little black dress, and that was the best advice her friend ever gave her. The second she entered Christian's apartment, he stood in shock. She looked ravishing in her little black dress. His hands found their way around her waist, and he immediately kissed her. His hands held her softly, yet tightly at the same time. He held her close to him as his hands lowered themselves. He lifted her thigh up and pinned her against a wall. His waist pressed into hers. His lips lowered from her lips to her jawline, then to her neck. Joanna had to bite her lip from crying out— the walls between Christian's apartment and his neighbors were extremely thin, and she really didn't want his neighbors bothering them. Joanna grabbed at the collar of his shirt with one hand and grasped his shoulder with the other. She could feel her legs giving out. Christian lifted her up and took her to the bedroom, his lips still pressed firmly against her skin.

Christian always seemed perfect in Joanna's eyes in every aspect. He knew exactly what to do to make her toes curl in excitement and her knees tremble. He was passionate. Joanna never had a lover like him before. With other guys, it felt like everything was about them finishing, but with Christian, she had never felt such love before. It felt like everything in that moment was about her and her own pleasure. For the first time in her life, Joanna finished before her partner did. It was riveting, and she actually enjoyed her experience.

After that fifth date, they spent many more restless nights together. Joanna would go to Christian's place often, and she would spend the night often. At some point, their meetups became a habit. If Joanna's friends didn't know where she was, then they would assume she was at Christian's. Dahlia learned to not call later in the day because Joanna would just ignore her. Christian and Joanna spent most of their free time together, and it was simply perfect. The way he held her hand was perfect, the way he hugged her was perfect, the way he kissed her was perfect, and the night they spent together after their fifth date was perfect. Christian was perfect— he was perfect for her. He was everything she could ever want.

"I'm going to Barcelona after this semester," Joanna told him one night— they were lying in bed together. It was dark, and moonlight entered the room. Christian was gazing down at Joanna, who was embraced in his arms. She covered up her bare collarbones just a bit with the bedsheets as she said, "I get to work as an understudy for one of my favorite fashion designers."

"That's good for you," Christian smiled at her; Joanna blushed.

"It would be nice if you could come with me," Joanna sighed as she wrapped her arms around Christian.

"I'll talk to some of the higher-ups in the company and see if there are any openings in the Barcelona branch," Christian thought out loud. "080 Barcelona Fashion would probably need more coverage this year."

Joanna looked up at the boy expectantly. Christian looked down at her face and kissed her forehead lightly. She was beaming at the boy as she told him, "I love you."

Christian only smiled back.

II

BARCELONA

Let it be whatever God wants it to be.
My crime is the stupidity of ignoring
that there are heartless people.
And it's burning, it's burning me and it burns me.

Y, ¿SI FUERA ELLA? — ALEJANDRO SANZ

BARCELONA, SPAIN

Joanna realized that her honeymoon period with Christian ended as soon as she found out more about him. It wasn't that he was a bad person, but they had nothing in common although they both were in the same industry. She was more interested in fashion while he only seemed to care for politics in the fashion world. She liked dogs while he was more of a cat person. She liked cuddling, and he only seemed to be interested in having sex.

The Christian she knew in Paris was different than the Christian she knew in Barcelona. Paris Christian was romantic, sweet, and perfect; Barcelona Christian was dry, cold, and the opposite. Maybe she should've been listening to him on those many dates she went on with him in Paris. If she had listened, would she have realized that he wasn't her soulmate earlier on? Would she have realized earlier that he was not as perfect as he seemed?

She realized how he was one night at dinner by the ocean side. Her first hint should've been the fact that she had to make the reservations for the place, and her second hint should've been when he came into the restaurant almost an hour late. Joanna didn't even realize that he was an hour late because she was so engrossed in a conversation with Dahlia. Her third hint was when she realized that he was not as perfect as he seemed because he was messy— and Christian was never messy in front of her.

"Christian," Joanna said rather quietly as they ate. "Why did you button your shirt up wrong?"

"What?" Christian looked down at his shirt, and sure enough, he missed a hole, so his shirt was on wrong. "Sorry, I was rushing. I got out of work late."

"What do you mean you got out of work late? I thought you said you finished your article," Joanna set down her utensils carefully.

"I had to send out a couple more emails," Christian sighed. "I told you I would be working late today."

"You write articles, for crying out loud!" Joanna had to refrain from raising her voice up a decibel. "You normally sit in the bedroom and write, so why are you suddenly going out to work?"

"Just because it isn't fashion week, it doesn't mean that I don't have work to finish. I'm trying to work my way up the ladder," Christian explained.

"Okay, then what were you working on that was so important that you came late and didn't even wear your shirt properly?" Joanna crossed her arms over her chest.

Christian was silent. Joanna looked down at her plate of food. She didn't have an appetite, which was apparent by the way her food was tossed about on the plate. She took the napkin off her lap, placed it on the table, and called the waiter over. She asked for the bill, and as the waiter left, she got her purse and started talking out her wallet.

"Joanna, what are you doing?" Christian asked.

"I'm paying the bill and leaving," Joanna said quietly. "I don't feel like eating."

The waiter came with the bill, and Joanna paid for the meal in cash before getting up and taking off. She waited for a taxi outside the restaurant when Christian came running out from the restaurant. He grabbed Joanna's wrist and asked, "What the hell? Why did you do that?"

"Christian, let go, it hurts," Joanna tried to get out of Christian's grip, but he only tightened it.

"You need to tell me why you did that," Christian said.

A taxi came to a stop by the curb, and Joanna managed to shake Christian off her as she got into the taxi. Joshua stood at the curb as she closed the door to the taxi and told the driver her address. She felt numb when she got home. She didn't know what it was, but there was definitely something wrong with Christian. She sat on the sofa in their apartment for quite a while and just thought about her image of her seemingly perfect Christian.

Christian got home later that night. He joined Joanna on the sofa and just looked at her. Joanna looked at him as well, and when she looked into his eyes, she couldn't even tell who he was anymore. When Christian looked into Joanna's eyes, he saw sadness. He held her hand and looked at their hands as Joanna let out a small sigh.

"Christian, can you answer a question for me?" Joanna asked slowly.

Christian nodded and held Joanna's hand just a little tighter; Joanna had to refrain from flinching.

"What's your favorite color?" she asked.

"Gray," he responded.

Joanna nodded. She couldn't tell him that she imagined him bathed in shades of pinks and periwinkles; he would disagree with her. She exhaled and looked at their hands. His hands used to be so familiar, but for some reason, she could barely recognize them now. Christian pulled his hands away from Joanna's hand and pulled her into a hug. She let herself get engulfed in his scent, only to realize that his scent wasn't even familiar either. Paris Christian smelt like cinnamon and peaches, but Barcelona Christian smelt like vanilla and honey. She definitely didn't know Christian anymore. Joanna escaped his embrace and went off into their bedroom. She closed the door gently behind her, a single tear rolling down her cheek as she realized she did not know the boy she loved anymore.

Joanna finished removing her makeup. She looked at the chain dangling on her neck. It was the marigold Christian had given her on their fourth date. She never took it off after he gave it to her. She sighed as she left the bathroom and went to the bed to see that Christian was already passed out in bed. She looked at him and inhaled slowly before sighing. She sat down on the bed and looked out the window in their room. The night sky was gorgeous, but Christian never seemed to appreciate it. She wished he appreciated the midnight sky. Joanna got under the covers and forced herself to sleep despite the unbearable distance between her and her love.

Joanna couldn't sleep all night. She kept rubbing the pendant between her thumb and pointer finger as she stared at the ceiling. She was up until the sunrise, and she watched as Christian woke up in time to watch the sunrise. She turned and looked at him gazing at the orange sky, and she asked, "Do you like the sunrise, Christian?"

Christian turned around and smiled at the girl. He nodded as he said, "The sunrise is gorgeous every morning here in Barcelona."

Joanna nodded. She got out of bed and said, "I'm going to go get ready for work. I'll see you when I get back home."

Although she was at work, Joanna couldn't focus at all. It felt as if someone told her that her whole life was a lie. In fact, she was so out of focus that her mentor told her to go home early that day. She got home and hung her keys on the hook next to the door as she walked in and closed the door behind her. She went to the bedroom and expected to see Christian working at his desk, but he was nowhere to be found. She looked around for him. He wasn't home. Joanna sat on her bed, defeated. It felt like all Christian cared for was his work and that she didn't mean as much to him. She felt neglected.

Joanna ended up going to bed when she got home. She wanted to take a nap, but she ended up sleeping through the rest of the day and the night. When she woke up the next morning, she was alone. Christian didn't return that night. Joanna started getting suspicious. Was Christian really just busy with work, or was he cheating on her?

That day, Joanna didn't have to go into work. She stayed at home and just browsed the internet. She wanted to text Christian, but her mind was reeling. She didn't know what to text him. She checked her phone to see if he texted her, but there wasn't a single message on her phone. Suddenly, an idea popped into her head. She checked the website of the company that Christian worked for to see if any of his articles were up. There were many articles, but there was only one recent article. It was about Barcelona fashion in general. Joanna bit her lower lip. She didn't want to baselessly accuse him of cheating on her, but at this point, she was almost certain that he was.

Instead of texting him, Joanna decided to call Christian. Her call immediately went to voicemail. She tried to call again, and this time her phone call went through. Christian picked up. He sounded out of breath.

"What?" he asked.

Joanna winced at the tone of his voice. He sounded curt, angry.

"Hey, where were you last night?" Joanna asked softly.

"I was busy working," Christian answered.

"Oh, I see," Joanna nodded and bit her lower lip. "Are you working out?"

"Yes. I'll talk to you later," Christian said before hanging up.

Joanna tried to say bye, but Christian ended the phone call before she could. Joanna was despondent. She wanted to cry, but she had to keep her mind level. She decided to take a walk. A long walk. She needed to clear her head. She would figure out the Christian situation later.

By the time Joanna got home, it was almost nine in the evening. She left her apartment a little after three in the afternoon. The apartment was dark, but Christian was definitely home. There were pots and pans in the kitchen that weren't out beforehand, and his keys were on the coffee table in the living room. She went to the bedroom and expected to see Christian working at his desk, only to see him in bed with bruises all over his bare chest. He was fast asleep. Joanna cleared her throat, and Christian's eyes opened. He sat up in bed and covered his chest with the blanket as he said, "Joanna, you're home early."

"What's with all the bruises on your chest?" she asked quietly; she was angry.

"I, uh," Joshua searched for an excuse.

Joanna walked towards the bed and snatched the blanket away to see that Christian had the same small bruises all over his torso. She looked at him angrily, tears welling up in her eyes. She asked him, "Are you cheating on me"

"No! No, I'm not cheating on you," Christian said slowly.

"Then why are there hickies all over your chest?" Joanna pointed out.

"Joanna, it's not what it looks like—" Christian started.

"What is it then? Are you going to tell me that you fell on some rocks and got these bruises?" Joanna questioned.

"No, I just... I made a mistake," Christian trailed off.

"So you are cheating on me," Joanna concluded.

"Listen, I was drunk, and one thing led to another," Christian had to stop himself.

The two of them were silent for a while. Joanna crossed her arms over her chest and she asked him, "Christian Lee, what do you think we are?"

"We're dating, of course," Christian said.

"I'm your girlfriend, then, right?" Joanna clarified.

"Yes, you are, and I am your boyfriend," Christian said.

"Then why did you cheat on me? Aren't we exclusively seeing each other? Do you not love me?" Joanna was on the verge of tears.

Christian pursed his lips. Joanna's eyes widened as she realized for the first time since Paris that Christian never told her he loved her back. She told him she loved him, and he only smiled. She scoffed and looked up at the ceiling as she ran her trembling fingers through her hair. She took a second to collect herself and gain enough confidence to make sure her voice didn't shake as she asked, "Why did you come to Barcelona with me? Why did you come to Barcelona, Christian?"

Christian looked down at the bedsheets in his lap. He didn't say a single word. Joanna just looked at him and nodded. She didn't say another word either. Christian got up out of bed and got dressed before leaving the apartment. The second the door closed, Joanna broke down. She sat down on the edge of the bed and cried her heart out as she finally,

finally came to realize that Christian was gone. Paris Christian was merely a figment of her imagination. She lost him in Barcelona.

The next day, Joanna woke up to see that Christian had taken all of his belongings and left. She was left all alone in her apartment in Barcelona. She came to Barcelona with her soulmate, the love of her life, but her feelings were never reciprocated. She brought her knees to her chest and cried to herself about the boy she once loved, the boy she now lost.

III

SEATTLE

I'm tired everyday
I'm thirsty for the rain
That waters all of my melodies
The needle in the skies
Never fails to light my night
And it sews my heart
On my tattered sleeve

SEATTLE — SAM KIM

SEATTLE, WASHINGTON

"Joanna, I need help with the documents for the shop," Dahlia said as she barged into Joanna's office.

"Put it on my desk. I'll go through them after I finish this email," Joanna pointed at a corner on her desk.

"Thank you, you're a lifesaver," Dahlia gushed as she placed the documents on the desk and kissed the top of Joanna's head.

Joanna smiled at the girl before returning to her computer monitor. It had been about three years since she returned from Barcelona, and although the experience was good for her, Joanna decided that she liked living in the States better mainly because it was more comfortable for her after the nightmare she experienced in Paris and Barcelona. After their graduation from their respective colleges, the two girls had met up again in Seattle, Washington. Dahlia graduated with a degree in business management while Joanna graduated with a degree in fashion design.

Dahlia and Joanna ran several businesses together, all of which were very successful. They made a lot of profit, and they were able to live their lives to the fullest, but since they were so busy with work, they didn't have the time to go out and meet other people. Well, at least that's what Joanna thought until Dahlia introduced her to her new boyfriend. She even vividly remembered when Dahlia introduced him because she was thoroughly surprised at how similar he was to her ideal type.

"I would appreciate it if you finished those documents quickly," Dahlia said as she popped into the office for a quick second. "Johnny is waiting on those documents."

"I know, I'm getting through them," Joanna said before making sure Dahlia closed the door.

Joanna picked up the documents that Dahlia left and answered the information that it asked for as she remembered how she and Dahlia even met Johnny in the first place. They decided to combine their businesses— Dahlia started a coffee shop, and Johnny owned a pastry shop next door. Now, the three of them were business partners. It was good and all, but Joanna wished she could find her own perfect significant other just as Dahlia did. She sighed as she finished the documents and got up from her chair. She left her office and went to Dahlia's office only to open the door on her and Johnny getting way too close for comfort.

"Ahem, I have your urgent document, Johnny," Joanna said loudly.

The two separated instantly, and they both cleared their throats as Johnny quickly got the documents from Joanna, thanked her, and left the office. Joanna turned to Dahlia and smiled at the embarrassed girl as she said, "Is that why you wanted me to do the documents?"

"No," Dahlia shook her head. "You were taking a while, though, so

Johnny suggested it."

Joanna chuckled and said, "Listen, I'm going to go out for a bit. Research if you will. You and Johnny can go back to being freaky."

Before Dahlia could retort, Joanna left the room as quickly as possible and ran to her office to get her coat. She put on her coat, grabbed her purse, and scurried out into the streets of Seattle.

December in Seattle was cold, but there wasn't snow, not that Joanna expected any snow because it rarely snowed in Seattle. Despite this, she didn't mind the weather in Seattle. She actually grew rather fond of Seattle after spending three years in the city. She liked the atmosphere of the city. It wasn't perfect, but it was nice, and that was all Joanna could ask for. She roamed the city for a bit to get a breath of fresh air and then walked over to the coffee shop that she, Dahlia, and Johnny owned to stop and warm up.

Upon entering the store, the baristas recognized Joanna and waved at her. They immediately provided her with a cup of coffee, and Joanna sat down at what she deemed her table in the corner of the shop to catch up on some emails that she received on her walk.

As Joanna sat and scrolled through her phone, she didn't realize how many customers were going in and out of the store, and she didn't realize that a person had walked up to her and was standing before her until she heard the person tap on the wooden table with his nails and cleared his throat. She looked up and immediately had the urge to flee, but she maintained her self control and managed to smile at him.

"Hi, Christian," Joanna said with a near-trembling voice.

"Hi, Joanna. It's been a while," he said as he smiled at her. He waited for a split second before asking, "May I sit here?"

Joanna could only nod, and Christian sat down. She stared at the figure before her and relived the nightmare that was Barcelona before her longing feelings for Paris returned. One of the baristas came by and gave Christian his coffee, Joanna snapping out of her trance as the barista set the mug down on the table.

"So, what have you been up to?" Christian asked as he picked up the mug.

"I started a couple of businesses with my friends. I actually own this coffee shop," Joanna managed to spit out. "What about you?"

Joanna tried to keep a smile on her face as Christian said, "Well, I work for Vogue now, but I'm in the area for a vacation. Nobody told me the weather in Seattle during the wintertime was this bad!"

Christian started laughing, and Joanna found it excruciatingly hard to laugh as well. She chuckled and said, "Yeah, well the weather here is like that."

"You live here now? How has that been?" Christian took a sip of his coffee.

"It's been nice. Dahlia actually came out here and forced me to come here after," Joanna couldn't bring herself to continue. She just trailed off and smiled.

"That's nice that you like it here. New York City is busy, but it's a great place," Joshua said.

"I know, Dahlia would not shut up about it when she was studying over there. Now she can't shut up about her boyfriend," Joanna smiled at the thought of Dahlia with Johnny.

"What about you? Are you with anyone at the moment?" Christian asked.

"No," Joanna sighed. "Busy with work, after all. What about you?"

"I'm actually engaged," Christian said a little too happily.

Joanna glanced at his left hand, and sure enough, there was a gold band wrapped around his ring finger. Joanna's smile faltered as she said, "That's nice. I'm sure you two are happy together."

"We are," Christian nodded.

The two sat in awkward silence before a sudden notification startled both of them. Christian took his phone out of his pocket and said, "That was my fianceé. I got to go. It was nice running into you!"

Joanna didn't say anything. She just watched as Christian left and met up with a gorgeous woman, his fianceé, and walked away from her as if nothing happened. She just gawked as he left, and she was left feeling numb again. She couldn't bring herself to finish her drink. She couldn't bring herself to even freaking laugh it off. She was numb. She continued looking out the window, and a snowflake floated down before her. She gazed at the lone snowflake as more joined and fluttered to the ground.

A tear slipped out of her eye as she watched the floating snow drift on. More tears leaked out of her eyes as she scrolled through her contacts and got to Dahlia's number.

"Joanna? What's up?" Joanna heard Dahlia say.

"Dahlia," Joanna cried out.

"Stay right there. I'm on my way," Dahlia said.

Dahlia stayed on the line as Joanna cried her heart out. A couple of the baristas came to comfort her as she continued crying out the feelings she suppressed for the past three years. Dahlia came running into the shop and embraced Joanna as she cried and cried about losing Christian.

"How could he just reappear like that in front of me? It hurts," Joanna sniffled.

"I know, Joanna, I know," Dahlia smoothed the girl's hair out.

"It's not fair, Dahlia. I loved him," Joanna started crying again.

"I know, but Joanna, you need to move on," Dahlia hugged Joanna tighter.

"I know," Joanna echoed.